LEPRECHAUN
on the
LOOse

ANNETTE KELLEHER

Illustrated by Philip Morrison

THE O'BRIEN PRESS
DUBLIN

This edition published 2001 by The O'Brien Press Ltd,
20 Victoria Road, Dublin 6, Ireland.
Tel: +353 1 4923333; Fax: +353 1 4922777
E-mail: books@obrien.ie
Website: www.obrien.ie

First published 2000 by Margaret Hamilton Books,
PO Box 28, Hunters Hill NSW 2110 Australia

ISBN: 0-86278-729-7

British Library Cataloguing-in-Publication Data
Kelleher, Annette
Leprechaun on the loose. - (Red flag ; 7)
1.Leprechauns - Juvenile fiction 2.Children's stories
I.Title II.Morrison, Phillip
823.9'14[J]

1 2 3 4 5 6 7 8 9 10
01 02 03 04 05 06 07

The O'Brien Press receives
assistance from

Layout and design: The O'Brien Press Ltd.
Illustrations: Phillip Morrison
Colour separations: C&A Print Services Ltd.
Printing: Cox & Wyman Ltd.

Contents

1. How It Started

Even for a leprechaun, Biddy Blatherskate was no great beauty. When you met her the word *nose* popped into your head and refused to leave. This was because most of the space on her face was occupied by a nose which would have looked perfectly at home on an inquisitive old man but was totally out of place on a small girl.

Anyway, one miserable day, when drizzling rain was falling soundlessly like tears from a sad grey eye, Biddy was sitting on a smooth rock staring into a pot of gold.

'If I could, I'd trade this rotten gold for a week of sunshine,' she grumbled, to nobody in particular.

'Would you indeed?' queried an interested voice.

'I would,' said Biddy, so lost in her grumbling she didn't realise that a real voice had answered her.

'Go on then, put your money where your nose is, I mean, where your mouth is!' The voice dropped out of a tree. It was wearing red shorts, a black T-shirt, and running shoes so caked in mud that half of County Kerry could have been lodged between the treads.

'Who are you?' Biddy quickly sat on the pot of gold. Her father had warned her not to take her eyes off it, not ever, and it was awfully hard to keep one eye on this strange creature with a small haystack on his head and the other on her treasure.

'I'm Corey!' the voice said.

'You mean Carey, I suppose,' Biddy corrected him.

'No! I mean Corey, Dumbo.'

'I've heard of Carney and Carey and Casey and Cornelius but never Corey Dumbo,' said Biddy, with a puzzled expression on her nose. 'What does it mean?'

'I don't know!' Corey shrugged his shoulders. 'Does it have to mean anything? It's just a stupid name.'

'My name is Biddy, short for Brigid who was a fire-goddess and it means strength,' Biddy explained proudly.

'Big Woop!' Corey said. 'Now, about this deal. You said you'd trade that pot of gold for a week of sunshine and I can give you the week of sunshine.'

'You talk funny,' Biddy giggled, moving uneasily on the gold because a particularly big coin was giving her a wedgie.

'Have you listened to yourself lately?' Corey looked offended. 'Anyway, I'm an Australian.'

'I've heard of aliens before.' Biddy's nose twitched with excitement. 'But I never thought one would hop out of a blackthorn tree and try to steal my pot of gold. Shouldn't you be wearing a spacesuit or something? Your skin is kind of brown. In fact you look a bit like an old peeled spud.' She giggled again.

'Australian!' Corey enunciated. 'You know, the land down under, Vegemite, koalas, kangaroos?'

'I've heard of kangaroos but never Austr-aliens,' Biddy said. 'I once saw Skippy on TV.'

'Well, for a pot of gold I'll show you one in real life.'

'Is that a fact?' said Biddy, stroking her chin just the way her father did when an interesting proposition came up for consideration.

'It is,' said Corey, thinking of all the gleaming coins in the pot under Biddy. 'I could show you a hundred kangaroos and guarantee you a week of sunshine. Australia is the driest continent on earth, you know. It doesn't rain for weeks, months, sometimes years.'

'Amazing,' said Biddy, looking up at the curdled, lumpy clouds overhead. 'In that case Ireland must be the wettest continent on earth,' she said miserably, ' because here it *rains* for weeks, months, sometimes years. It gives me rain depression.'

'How would you like to spend a week on a beach as white as snow and swim in an ocean as blue as ...' Corey looked around for a comparison but Ireland on that day had only two colours – bright, soggy green and dull, soggy grey.

'The ocean is not blue,' Biddy shivered. 'I once visited the Atlantic ocean and it was a grey, dark, hissing, spitting monster with lots of slimy black hands waiting to drag me off to be eaten at Neptune's table.'

'Not our ocean,' Corey contradicted. 'Our ocean is as blue as ... my eyes,' he said, for want of a better comparison.

Biddy leaned forward a little to get a good look at the alien's eyes.

'Does it have a black island in the middle?' she asked.

'What?' Corey snapped. Patience wasn't his strong point and the rain trickling down his neck was making him twitchy and even more eager to be off with the gold.

'Does your ocean have a black island in the middle?' Biddy asked, water dripping from the end of her nose like a tap needing a new washer.

'Would you like one?' Corey asked.

'Well, it would be handy if I got tired of swimming and wanted to have a rest.'

'Done!' said Corey. 'You can swim in an ocean as blue as my eyes and rest on the black island in the middle.'

'Will the island have kangaroos and vegemites running around on it?' Biddy leaned forward again. She was getting more interested in this deal by the minute and even if the boy was giving her a load of blarney, at least it was helping to pass away a rainy day.

'Vegemites?' Corey scoffed. 'Vegemite doesn't run around. Vegemite is dark brown, smelly, stuff. You spread it on toast.'

'What does it taste like, this Vegemite?' Biddy asked.

'I don't know. It's not like anything. It's just Vegemite.'

'Have you got some?'

'No! Like I'm really going to go around with a jar of Vegemite in my pocket,' Corey snorted.

'I go around with a pot of gold.' Biddy sniffed.

'You're a nerd then, aren't you?' Corey said. 'If I had a pot of gold I'd put it in a bank.'

'Bad move.' Biddy shook her head so furiously that a swish of water flew into the four winds. 'One of my ancestors put his gold in a nice mossy bank and it took three generations to find it again.'

Corey shook his own blonde haystack in dismay. 'Look, are you interested in a week of sunshine in exchange for that pot of gold, or not?' he asked.

'I'll sleep on it,' Biddy said, not wanting to jump into an unfamiliar briar patch without first examining the landscape.

'That's cool!' Corey said, feeling anything but cool under the collar. 'I'll come back tomorrow at noon. You can let me know your decision then.'

'Fair enough!' Biddy agreed. Clutching the pot of gold in her two strong arms, she headed off in a westerly direction, knowing full well that her house lay to the east.

2. How It Continued

Biddy slept badly. With a lumpy pot of gold under your head and a nose which needed its own pillow, you'd sleep badly too.

When she awoke in the morning there was gold everywhere, including a small coin inside her ear.

'A thousand curses on this rotten gold!' Biddy tried to poke the coin out of her ear.

But Biddy's short, fat fingers were too big to fit in her ear, even though they went easily up her nose. Her mother said that one day she'd pick her brain out. Biddy imagined an enormous grey thing like a boiled pork sausage coming out, which made nose picking dangerous and even more exciting, so she wasn't deterred at all.

So, as her finger was too big for her ear, Biddy had to borrow one of her mother's hairpins.

Having rescued that coin she flicked a few others out from underneath her. They pinged across the slate floor.

'Biddy! Are you minding the gold?' her mother called from the kitchen. 'If you lose any of it your father will throttle you.'

'Of course I'm minding it.' Biddy hopped out of bed and snatched up the coins. 'I shouldn't have to mind it,' she whisper-grumbled. 'I should have a brother to mind it. Gold sitting is boy's work.'

'Well, you don't have a brother.' Her mother had ears that could hear butterfly wings moving on another continent. 'If we had a boy I daresay he'd be delighted to look after the gold, but since we don't, it's your responsibility for the moment and it would be nice if you did it without complaining.'

'When is Da coming home?' Biddy demanded.

'When he finds your grandfather's gold,' her mother answered.

'And when will that be?' Biddy asked her grumpy, stumpy reflection in a long oval mirror.

The reflection flared its nostrils and poked out a short red tongue with a channel down the middle before slumping its shoulders with a resigned sigh and saying quietly, 'When you're bent and old like your grandmother.'

'Mocking is catching,' her mother said crossly.

Biddy climbed back into bed and pulled the clothes up to her chin. It seemed to her that leprechauns would be better off without any gold. She certainly wouldn't miss it. Ever since her grandfather had misplaced his pot, Biddy had been lugging her father's pot around twenty-four hours a day and she was sick of it.

'Biddy!' Her mother came into the bedroom. She was dressed in her going-out clothes – a green coat with a fur-trimmed hood, black patent boots and a black handbag. 'I have to go and look after your grandmother for a week. She's caught one of those nasty human diseases. Her nose is leaking all over the place and she's trying to blow out the fire with gusts of wind that come unexpectedly out of her mouth.'

'Sneezing!' Biddy said.

'Rubbish, it's not freezing at all. It's too wet for freezing.' Her mother frowned at the pile of discarded clothes on top of the bed, the muddy boots under the bed and the untidy child in the bed. 'Now, can I trust you to look after everything while I'm away?' she asked. 'I'd take you with me but you stress your grandmother out with your shenanigans.'

'I don't want to go,' Biddy said. 'Grandma is ...' She was going to say a smelly, cranky old sourpuss, but her mother's bad eye was fixed firmly on her. 'Grandma is going to need lots of peace and quiet,' she said instead. 'I'll be fine here.'

'You will wash up occasionally and not bury all the dishes in the garden like you did last time?'

'Yes, Ma!'

'You will look after the gold, won't you?'

'Couldn't you take it for a week?' Biddy asked. 'You could put it under Grandma's pillow. Nobody would touch it there.' Then she thought, *not without having lots of sharp false teeth injected into them.*

'No!' her mother replied.

'Please!' Biddy pleaded. 'I want to play for a change.'

'You're not responsible enough to play tricks on people,' her mother snorted, as if the very idea was outrageous.

'Then how come I'm responsible enough to look after the stupid gold?'

'Don't be nosy ... cheeky, I mean,' her mother warned, taking a step closer to the bed.

'I wasn't! I didn't!' Biddy covered her ears.

'Is it all there?' her mother demanded, peering into the pot of gold.

'Yes, Ma! I counted it yesterday.'

That was a lie. Biddy couldn't be bothered to count the gold. She always got distracted and had to start over and over again. Besides, she thought her parents worried too much about the stuff. As if there was nothing more important in life, like basking in warm sunshine.

Sunshine! The coin dropped. Biddy sat bolt upright. The Austr-alien was coming back at noon. Her mother was going away for a week. Biddy could clear two beehives with one puff of smoke. She could get a minder for the gold, have a week of warm sunshine and still be back home with the gold when her parents returned.

Hopping gingerly out of bed she began spitting on the biggest coin she could find and polishing it with the tail of her nightshirt. 'Nice gold, isn't it?'

she said, holding it up for her mother's inspection. 'This one is my favourite.'

Her mother raised her eyes to the ceiling. 'Heaven protect us,' she said. 'Guard it, don't love it, or you'll be just like your father.'

That idea seemed to please her anyway, because she smiled and patted Biddy on the head. 'You'll be all right then?' she said. 'And I'm just on the other side of the hill if you need me.'

'I'll be fine,' Biddy said, picking up her mother's bag and escorting her to the front door. 'Don't worry about a thing.'

'You're a good girl ... most of the time,' her mother said.

'Bye, Ma!' Biddy shut the door and did a little hornpipe around the kitchen floor. Then she dressed in her best clothes, buried her cereal bowl in the garden, borrowed her father's best hat and went to sit on the smooth rock under the blackthorn tree to wait for the alien.

3. How the Plan was Hatched

'What kept you?' Biddy demanded when Corey showed up, not at noon, not an hour after noon, but midway through the afternoon when the sun was already putting on its slippers and thinking of bed. Not that you could see the sun, because it was raining again. Not soft, drizzling rain either, but cold, pelting rain that was flung into your face like a fistful of wet sand.

Biddy looked, and felt, like a drowned rat. Her temper spluttered like an untended pot of porridge.

'Sorry!' said Corey, not sounding at all apologetic, and dry as a bone inside a long, brown coat, wellington boots and a wide-brimmed hat. 'Our car got bogged and we had to wait for someone to rescue us.'

'Stupid aliens!' Biddy muttered. 'If you've got so much sunshine, Vegemite, kangaroos and blue skies in Australia, why don't you stay there, instead of coming over here bogging our cars and inconveniencing us?'

'You *are* in a foul mood.' Corey flopped down beside Biddy, who was trying to shelter under a large tree root. 'What you need is a holiday in the sun. Have you made a decision yet about the gold?'

'Maybe I have,' replied Biddy, not wanting to sound too enthusiastic. 'How much longer are you going to be in Ireland?'

'One week! Well, one week and one day to be exact,' said Corey. 'We're visiting my Irish grandfather. What have you got in mind?'

Now, sitting in the rain for several hours had washed some of the sludge out of Biddy's brain. She'd had plenty of time to think about the consequences of her actions if she turned up in front of her father without the gold. So she'd hit on a plan – not a brilliant one, but it was the best she could do at short notice. Besides, she'd been studying the *Dictionary of Leprechaun Business Practices*, paying particular attention to the sections on 'Human Frailties' and 'Coveted Possessions'.

'Do you have lots of money?' she asked.

'Nah! D'you think I'd be interested in your pot of gold if I had heaps of money?'

'The *DLBP* says that humans never have enough money,' Biddy said.

'DLPB?' Corey wrinkled his nose.

'Never mind,' Biddy said. 'Do you have a driver's licence?'

'Do I look old enough to drive a car?'

'Old enough to get one bogged,' she sniggered.

'That was my father,' Corey said. 'And it wasn't his fault – your roads are so narrow that there isn't even room for two cars to pass each other.'

'Well, isn't that a good thing?' Biddy said. 'Imagine how many stupid aliens would get bogged if the roads were wider? Now, do you have credit cards?'

'No!'

'Do you have *anything* valuable?' Biddy demanded.

'I have a passport,' Corey said. 'But it's so important that my father won't even allow me to carry it.'

'That's the very thing I'm after then.' Biddy clapped her hands. 'Give me your passport and I'll be off to Australia for a week while you stay here and look after the gold.'

'I can't!' Corey jumped to his feet. 'My passport is like my ticket home. Without it I could be stuck here for ever. Anyway, don't you have a passport of your own?'

'Be real!' Biddy snorted. 'Leprechauns aren't recognised as real people. Who'd give me a passport?'

'But my passport wouldn't be of any use to you. You don't even look like me,' Corey said. 'The immigration people would take one look at your nose ... I mean face, and the game would be up.'

'Just leave that part to me,' Biddy said, not letting on that she could take any shape she desired, even disappear into thick air if she wanted to.

'I don't know.' Corey dug a little trench in the mud with the edge of his boot. 'My father would kill me for giving away my passport.'

'*My* father would kill *me* for giving away the gold.'

'That's true, I suppose. But you see,' Corey lied, 'I have a better plan. Why don't I hide you in my suitcase and take you to Australia next week?'

'No! No! That's no good at all.' Biddy got up and paced around the pot of gold. 'My Ma is away this week. Next week she'll be back like a winter frost, looking for me and the gold. There will be hell to pay if we're missing. It's this week or not at all.'

Corey looked at the little pot of gold glistening under the gnarled tree roots. He wanted it badly, so badly that his hands were sweaty, so badly that he hadn't slept all night with the excited anticipation of all the things he could buy with it. A new surfboard, a mountain bike, stacks of CDs, anything he wanted.

'There must be another way,' he argued, his round, freckled face puckering like half an orange about to be squeezed. He wanted the gold without any complicated strings attached to it.

'There isn't,' said Biddy.

'How do I even know you'll be back in a week with my passport. You might like Australia and decide to stay there,' Corey said.

'Not without my pot of gold,' Biddy replied. 'I'd be back for my father's gold. Do you think I'm a complete idiot?'

Corey looked at the leprechaun. She seemed fair dinkum about the deal. If handing his passport over was the only way he could get his hands on the gold, then he supposed he'd just have to take the risk.

'All right,' he agreed reluctantly. 'I'll go back to the house and try to get my passport. I'll bring it here first thing tomorrow.'

'Fair enough!' said Biddy, who was trembling with cold.

'D'you want me to take the gold now, save you lugging it back home in the rain?' Corey offered.

'Get away with you!' Biddy chuckled. 'Do you think I came down the river on a bicycle? You'll get the gold when I get the passport.'

And they parted company for that day, Biddy to spend another uncomfortable night in bed with the gold and Corey to spend another night imagining the spending of it.

4. How the Exchange Took Place

The next morning the sun was shining, birds were singing, the fuchsias glistened like ripe berries and Biddy thought that maybe it wasn't so important to go to Australia after all. Instead of meeting Corey, she buried her cereal bowl, a bread plate, a knife and a spoon and went paddling in the river.

At lunchtime grey clouds came rolling across the sky like an ocean of bad temper on the prowl, and Biddy changed her mind.

Lugging the pot of gold under her jumper, she arrived at the blackthorn tree to find Corey pacing about angrily.

'Where were you?' Corey demanded. 'I could have been golfing with my father this morning. I'm supposed to be enjoying my holiday, not wasting my time out here, doing nothing.'

'I didn't stop you,' said Biddy. 'Have you got the passport?'

'Have you got the gold?'

'No, I've just grown this enormous carbuncle on my side,' Biddy said, prodding herself.

'Give me the gold and I'll give you the passport,' said Corey, pulling a small, blue book out of his pocket.

'Give me the passport and I'll give you the gold,' Biddy answered, pulling out the pot of gold.

Corey gazed at the gold. His eyes were so bright that Biddy could see the gold reflected in their ocean blueness. She imagined himself swimming to the island to watch the kangaroos.

'This is getting us nowhere,' Corey snapped impatiently. 'Don't you trust me or something?'

'About as much as you trust me,' Biddy countered.

'Okay! Put the gold into my right hand and I'll put the passport into your left hand,' Corey said.

'Both of my hands are right hands.' Biddy was indignant. 'What would be wrong with them?'

'Okay! Right hands! They're all right hands!' Corey said. 'Satisfied?'

'This pot of gold is too heavy for one right hand,' Biddy said. 'You might drop it.'

Corey looked up at the darkening sky and clenched his teeth.

'Listen carefully,' he said. 'I'm going to put my passport between my teeth. As soon as the pot of gold is in my hands, you can take the passport.'

'What if you won't let it go?' Biddy said suspiciously.

'I will! I will let it go. Cross my heart and hope to die if I don't.'

Biddy advanced. It was harder to hand over the gold than she had anticipated. She imagined her father dancing with fury at the sight, his face bulging like a boil about to burst and her mother wailing like a banshee at the loss of it.

But, she reasoned, the passport was her insurance. Corey would return the gold to get his passport back. After all, it was so precious that he was as reluctant to hand it over as Biddy was to hand over the gold.

Biddy snatched the passport and looked at the small photograph. 'This doesn't look anything like you,' she said.

'It looks even less like you,' Corey said. 'In fact, if you get through customs with that, I'll be a monkey's uncle.'

'A monkey would take a better photo,' Biddy said, sliding the passport into her pocket. She felt lighter already without the cumbersome gold.

'You must be back in exactly one week,' Corey said. 'I'll meet you here at noon next Friday.'

'You're sure it will be sunny in Australia?'

'Positive,' Corey said. 'I suppose you'll want a few of these coins to pay for your air fare?'

'Spend the gold!' Biddy shrieked. 'We never spend the gold.'

'So what do you do with it?'

'Nothing! We just mind it!'

'But why?' said Corey. 'You must use it for something.'

'That would be stupid, wouldn't it?' Biddy said. 'There's not much point in having gold if you're just going to spend it. Sure then it wouldn't be our gold any more. It would belong to someone else.'

'So how do you intend paying for your ticket to Australia?' Corey demanded. 'They cost a lot of money, you know.'

'I won't need one.' Biddy said.

'You're going to stow away?' Corey's eyes opened wide. 'You're going to stow away with my passport in your pocket. Holy sheet of tin! If you get caught my name will be splashed all over the newspapers.'

'I won't get caught,' Biddy said. 'Leprechauns don't exist, remember? Now guard that pot of gold with your life. I'll be back in one week.'

'But ... wait ... hang on ... if you're going to stow away you won't be needing my passport,' Corey argued.

'That's right!' Biddy grinned mischievously. And with that she hopped and skipped, as light as an evening breeze, across the hillside without a care in the world, leaving Corey with the burden of the gold.

5. How Corey Cared for the Gold

Corey wasted no more time on the side of the hill. It gave him the creeps now to be alone there, among the wild furze, with the whistling wind echoing between crags. His grandfather had said that fairies and leprechauns were devious creatures, quite capable of delivering serious maladies – shrivelled legs, humps, even death. Corey didn't really believe it, but still there was the slightest element of fear in his heart as he walked away with a whole pot of gold. Real gold. He ran his fingers over the solidness of it. It was no mirage. He was rich.

Bundling the gold into his jacket he hurried over the stony ground, twitching and glancing over his shoulder at the merest crackle. A crow swooping low over his head, uttering a loud 'caw', nearly made him wet himself. He was relieved when he saw the smoke curling out of his grandfather's chimney and the old man digging in the vegetable garden.

'What's that under your oxter?' the old man asked.

'What?' Corey had hoped to disappear before his grandfather had a chance to question him.

'Did you find some unexpected treasure?' His grandfather closed one eye against the glare of the afternoon light.

'It's nothing,' Corey said, scuttling into the small stone cottage. Sometimes his grandfather gave him the creeps too. He had a face like lichen-ridden old rock, and his two tiny, hawk-like eyes pierced into your face, scavenging. His grandfather didn't say much, but Corey suspected that he knew a lot and that he really was afraid of the fairies.

In the tiny upstairs bedroom, with the door closed behind him, Corey looked out on the barren hillside. It seemed hostile all of a sudden, with its exposed rocks and wind-whipped furze. He closed the curtains and sat on the iron bed. How would he hide the gold from his grandfather for a whole week? The old man was nosy. He had a habit of walking in at any time and he never knocked on doors.

Corey pulled the suitcase out from under his bed. He had no choice. He'd have to put the gold in there, pile clothes on top of it and hope that it would be safe. At least his father didn't pry.

For a while he lay on the bed and thought about the spending of the gold, and of his friends, how envious they would be of all the things he'd buy. How they would follow him around hoping to borrow his new toys. How he might sometimes treat them to tuckshop. How Angela Morris would change her mind about hating him when she saw how popular he'd become.

'Corey!' His father arrived home from golf. 'It's a nice day. Let's go for a ride. There's an old castle a few kilometres out of town. I'd like you to see it.'

'Is Grandfather coming?' Corey asked.

'No! I'm too stiff in the joints these days for bicycle riding,' his grandfather said, pulling a grimy pipe out of his pocket and tapping it on a fence post.

'Oh!' Corey licked his lips nervously. He was in a dilemma. He didn't want to leave the gold – not with his grandfather snooping around – but he couldn't possibly take it with him, and if he refused to go it would make the old man even more suspicious.

'Okay, Dad, I'm coming,' Corey said, stuffing shoes and a tennis racquet against the suitcase and closing the bedroom door.

That night Corey didn't sleep well. Rain splattered against the window pane, slates shuddered on the roof, unexpected noises creaked in the kitchen where the fire was dying. His grandfather never put the fire out before going to bed. In the morning he'd breathe life into a small nest of glowing embers and a new fire would be born.

Corey shivered under the mound of bedclothes. He wished now that he hadn't given Biddy his passport. He felt foolish for doing it. Maybe his grandfather was right. Maybe leprechauns were devious. Still, he had the pot of gold and nothing was going to make him give it back. Somehow, he'd trick Biddy out of the passport. If only he could keep his grandfather from getting too suspicious. The old man was more trouble than the leprechauns. If only the holiday would end so that they could go home to safety.

'Someone died last night,' Corey's grandfather said next morning, while slicing a loaf of soda bread. Black pudding and rashers of bacon sizzled in a frying pan behind him.

'Um?' Corey's dad said absentmindedly as he browsed through an old newspaper.

'How d'you know?' Corey asked, a small shiver running down his spine.

'Didn't ye hear the banshee wailing half the night?'

'Rubbish!' Corey's father said. 'That was only the wind howling on the hillside.'

Corey relaxed, glad that his father was nothing like Grandad.

'Mark my words,' the old man said, plucking the rashers from a pool of grease and cracking two eggs into it. 'Mark my words.'

That afternoon a funeral procession passed the house. Grandfather said nothing but there was a self-satisfied look on his craggy face. Corey's dad didn't seem bothered, but Corey felt the place closing in around him. He started noticing twinges of pain in his shin bones, and imagined that a small lump was growing on his spine.

He checked on the gold. It was there, looking a bit dull in the suitcase under the bed. Corey polished one coin and stuck it in his pocket.

'Where did you get this?' the shopkeeper asked when Corey tried to spend it.

'Why?'

'It's unusual. Never seen one like it before. Anyway, you can't spend it in my shop. It's not legal tender.'

The same thing happened in every shop. The gold was useless. He couldn't spend it. It was leprechaun's gold.

'A bit like fool's gold, I suppose,' Corey muttered, tossing it back in the pot.

The week dragged on. Corey lost his appetite.

He worried day and night about not getting his passport back, of being left in Ireland with his grandfather while his father returned to Australia. He wondered if he would ever get to spend the gold at all. Maybe he'd end up just minding it for ever while it gathered dust.

To make matters worse, it was raining again and all they could do was sit inside and watch the water dribbling down outside the glass, like three bored fish in a tank. Corey felt miserable. He had caught Biddy's rain depression.

6. How Biddy Fared in Australia

Meanwhile Biddy, having stowed away on a Qantas flight, had arrived in Brisbane on a particularly hot day. Having adopted a large family, she was on her way to Hervey Bay in an eight-seater van.

Presently she was occupying an empty seat at the back, occasionally popping into the seats in front of her to pinch food and lollies from the four children who seemed to be constantly eating. When they weren't eating they were squabbling. With Biddy interfering they were more quarrelsome than ever.

'You stole my black jellybaby!'

'Did not!'

'Did so!'

'Shush!' their mother said. 'You're distracting your father.'

'Shut your gobs!' Biddy whispered, stealing another jellybaby and retreating to the back seat to stuff her own gob and maybe have a little sleep.

'Would you look at that?' she pressed her face against the window of the van when they reached the bay. The beach wasn't quite as white as snow, but close enough, and the sea was indeed a kind of blue.

Biddy hopped out when the family stopped for fuel and ran across the road to the beach. She stopped briefly to look up at a sign. It said, SWIM BETWEEN THE FLAGS.

Biddy obeyed. It was hard work ploughing through the hot sand and soon her belly was grazed and her back was hot, so she ran and threw herself into the water to cool off. Then she went back to swim between the flags again, then plunged into the water to cool off. It was so much fun that she did it all afternoon, until she'd worked up a huge appetite.

'I wonder what the aliens eat?' she thought, and walked across the park to where a family was cooking something on a sheet of dirty-looking steel. It smelt enticing enough so she swiped what looked like a sausage and took a bite.

'Ugh! That's no sausage!' she spat it out on the grass. 'It must be something else, alien brains maybe?' Anyway, she wasn't eating that. She helped himself to a crusty bun instead and retreated under a bush to eat it. Then, being very tired and jet lagged, she fell asleep.

When she awoke the beach was deserted. A full moon bobbed about on the waves. Biddy felt uncomfortable, like someone had slapped a hot poultice on her back. Her head ached horribly and her bones were sore.

For the rest of the night she groaned and moaned and sweated and shivered. In the morning a scorching sun stepped blatantly out of the sea and she retreated further under the shady place to groan some more.

'What's wrong with you?' A boy with a laughing face crawled under the bushes to rescue a runaway ball.

'I dunno!' Biddy said. 'I think the fairies visited last night and tortured me. You do have fairies in Australia?'

'Don't think so!' the boy said. 'Only Aboriginal spirits. Pull up your shirt.'

'Nooooo!' Biddy pleaded. 'Don't touch me.'

'You're sunburnt. Really, really badly sunburnt. You're going to cop it.'

'Cop it?' Biddy groaned.

'Suffer!' The boy said. 'You'd better go home and put on sunscreen.'

'I can't go home, not for a week,' Biddy said. 'I came here to bask in the sun, to see kangaroos and to eat Vegemite.'

'If you bask in the sun any more you'll get skin cancer and die.'

'You lying devil!' Biddy said.

'I am not. Too much sun causes cancer, everyone knows that.'

'What's cancer?'

'A disease. It eats you up.'

'Sounds more like a monster,' Biddy frowned.

'Torren!' a woman's voice called.

'Who's torn?' Biddy asked.

'Me!' said the boy.

'You don't look torn,' Biddy said. 'Can't someone mend you?'

'Not torn, dumbo! Torren's my name. That's my mum calling me.'

'You aliens have weird names,' Biddy said. 'First Corey, now Torren, what next?'

'If you can't go home for a week you'd better come with me,' Torren said. 'I'll get you some cream for your sunburn.'

'What about your mother?' Biddy asked, knowing her own mother would have forty fits if she arrived home with a stranger.

'She's cool!' Torren said. 'She's a writer. She'll just think that a new character has moved in for a while.'

'All right so!' Biddy crawled to her feet and followed along behind Torren and his mother, like a very old woman.

For the rest of the week Torren was as good as his word. He got a whole tube of cream for Biddy's sunburn and together they watched television and played video games. Sometimes Torren went for a walk along the beach with his mother but Biddy didn't dare to poke her nose outside the door in case the sun monster got her. Besides, she didn't like the hot weather much. It made her sweat like a pig and she had to drink buckets of chlorinated water which made her feel quite sick.

At night she lay awake worrying about her father's pot of gold, hoping that Corey wasn't spending it and hoping that her mother hadn't come home early, or even worse that her father had come home.

On Biddy's last day in Australia, Torren came to the bedroom with a tray.

'What's that?' Biddy asked.

'Toast and Vegemite!' Torren said. 'You haven't seen any kangaroos but you'd better not leave without tasting Vegemite.'

Biddy was feeling pretty good. Her head had stopped throbbing and her bones had stopped aching. She picked up the bread and put it close to her nose.

'It smells weird,' she said.

'Taste it,' Torren said, popping a bit in his own mouth. 'It's yummy.'

Biddy took a bite, a big bite.

'What d'you reckon?' Torren asked.

'It's kind of wild.'

'And?'

'Bitter!'

'And?'

'It's poison! It's vile! It's making me want to vomit!' Biddy dived off the bed and ran to the bathroom.

'What a wimp!' Torren rolled around the bed. He laughed and rolled, and rolled and laughed so much that he fell off the bed on to the floor.

Biddy was not impressed about being poisoned. She left without saying goodbye and went to hitch a lift to the airport, with the midday sun beating down on her, fading her father's best hat.

'Oh, what I wouldn't give for a nice shower of rain,' Biddy said. 'I'll never complain about the weather again. The sooner I get home and collect my pot of gold the better I'll like it.'

And she hopped on the first available flight and curled up in a ball in the cockpit, right behind the pilot's seat. She stayed there without moving all the way home to Ireland, where it was raining cats and dogs, where the sky was as grey as the sea and the fields were green and cool and the sun monster was nowhere to be seen.

'Now to collect my pot of gold,' Biddy said, hopping and skipping all the way to Kerry.

7. How Complications Set In

'You look like a charred chicken,' Corey laughed when Biddy appeared at noon the following day.

'It's not funny!' said Biddy, whose skin was peeling, revealing pinker skin underneath. 'Soon my inside is going to be my outside and then how am I going to get on?'

'Oh, it's only sunburn,' Corey scoffed. 'I've been sunburnt heaps of times and it hasn't done me any harm.'

'You'll die,' Biddy warned.

'So will you,' Corey answered. 'Everyone will die sometime.'

'Not leprechauns,' Biddy said. 'Anyway, I've come for my pot of gold.' She was too tired to argue and her sense of humour had entirely disappeared.

'Didn't we make a deal?' Corey said. 'Didn't you get a week of sunshine?'

'One day!' Biddy said. 'And then I was burned to a cinder.'

'Didn't you get white beaches and blue seas?'

'There was no island in the middle and no kangaroos.'

'Didn't you get Vegemite?'

'Don't talk about it,' Biddy clutched her stomach. 'That awful poison nearly killed me.'

'I'd say you got a fair deal,' said Corey, who had no intention of parting with the gold. 'I'd say you should return my passport and we'll call it quits.'

'Passport?' Biddy felt her tongue swell and fill her mouth like a soggy slice of bread.

'Remember that little blue folder with my photo,' Corey said sarcastically. 'Give it to me and I'll be on my way.'

Biddy didn't need to feel in her pockets to know that the passport wasn't there. In fact she couldn't remember the last time she'd seen it. Maybe it was in the sand between the flags or floating in the blue ocean or maybe it was in Torren's house in Hervey Bay.

'You do have the passport?' Corey's chin twitched a bit and his eyes half closed.

'Course I do,' Biddy said. 'Hand me back my father's pot of gold and I'll give you the passport.'

'Do you think I was born under a cabbage leaf?' Corey laughed. 'Show me the passport.'

'I can't!'

'You'd better!'

'I lost it!'

'You what?'

'I think I lost it,' said Biddy, feeling quite foolish.

'You ... you nerd ... you idiot ... you small, insignificant lump of toad poo!' Corey's face went bright red. 'How could you lose my passport? Holy sheet of tin, my father will go ape over this.'

'I'm sorry!' Biddy said. 'I didn't mean to lose it.'

'Sorry! Didn't mean to! I thought leprechauns were smart!'

'We are,' Biddy said.

'Are not!'

'Are!'

Corey sat under the blackthorn tree, his head in his hands, the pot of gold between his thighs. Biddy sat opposite and peeled some dead skin off her arms.

'You could always stay here,' Biddy suggested. 'Ireland's not that bad.'

'It's not that good,' Corey said. 'It's always raining. Anyway, I'd like to go home and besides, I don't care much for my grandfather.'

'Me neither,' agreed Biddy. 'My grandfather tries to play tricks on me.'

'Like what?'

'Like once he tried to give me two heads and another time he tried to bury me alive.'

'Struth!' said Corey. 'My grandfather's not that bad. He tries to kill us with greasy rashers and black puddings and he spits a lot, big thick spits that look like oysters. You never know when he's going to do one, they just arrive beside you like missiles. He's very nosy too, and his stories give me the creeps. It's like living with Frankenstein's father.'

There was silence for a while. A low-flying crow sliced the air between them and Corey jumped.

'What are we going to do?' he said. 'I can't go home without my passport.'

'And I can't go home without my father's gold.'

So they sat and they sat and they sat some more and neither one could relieve the other's misery.

Night fell! One of those cold nights when the wind seems lonesome for company. It manages to penetrate under your arms and crawl up your nose. It whistles in one ear and out the other and the sky sends freezing darts from her starry slingshot.

'I'm hungry,' Corey said. 'Grandfather will be cooking bacon and cabbage and Dad will be reading the paper and wondering where I am.'

'Me too,' said Biddy. 'I'm as empty as a new coffin. My mother will be cooking for Grandma and my father will be looking for Grandad's pot of gold, I hope.'

'What are we going to do?' asked Corey.

'Don't know!' Biddy answered.

'You don't know much for a leprechaun,' Corey said.

'Nor you for an alien.'

And they sat and they sat, and they thought and they thought, but it didn't help.

About midnight a long mournful wailing came up one side of the hill.

'What was that?' Corey awoke with a start. 'Is someone dead? Is that the banshee?'

'Sounds more like my mother.' Biddy jumped to her feet. 'She's arrived home and is looking for me and the gold. Well, mostly the gold.'

'I'd better go then,' Corey said, grabbing the pot of gold and running down the other side of the hill towards his grandfather's cottage. He stumbled and staggered over and around rocks that were hunched like frozen warriors against the wind, leaving Biddy alone to face her angry mother.

8. How Corey Disposed of the Gold

The stone cottage was deserted. The fire was dying. The food was uneaten in the blackened pots. The newspaper was open on the table. The candle was flickering on the wide, stone windowsill.

Corey ran up the stairs and pushed the gold into his suitcase. His father had already packed in readiness for tomorrow's journey and the leather folder containing tickets and identification was lying on the small bedside cabinet.

Corey peered through the tiny window. He imagined he could see lights on the hillside, small moving lights, like those of a search party. The wailing seemed louder and more pitiful, and was getting closer and closer.

He was trapped.

If he stayed in the cottage the leprechauns would find a way in or else his grandfather would return and force him to give up the gold. Corey thought his grandfather was a cowardly man to be terrified of people a quarter of his size. He didn't know what his own father would say about the gold, but he was always trying to win Lotto. Wasn't that the same as trying to win a pot of gold?

Besides, Corey had struck a fair deal with Biddy, fair enough anyway. If only the stupid leprechaun hadn't gone and lost his passport.

The wailing was so close now that Corey thought they must be at the end of the small laneway that led to the house.

He panicked.

He grabbed the gold.

'I will not give it up,' he said aloud, running down the stairs. He opened the door and reached for one of the hired bicycles that were propped against the whitewashed wall. Carefully placing the gold, still wrapped in his jacket, into the basket, he hopped on the bike and pedalled furiously down the road.

He would find some way to hide the gold. If he couldn't keep it now he would put it somewhere safe and come back for it later when things had settled down.

9. How Biddy got an Earbashing

Meanwhile, Biddy was trudging down the hill, her two ears as red as hot coals and giving off just as much heat.

'I knew you couldn't be trusted with the gold,' her mother was yelling. 'You're nothing but a lazy, ignorant, good-for-nothing little brat. I told your father not to put the gold into your keeping but would he listen? Would he listen? No! And now this!'

'Sniff! Sniff!' said Biddy.

'Padraig, son of Diarmuid, your daughter the fire-goddess has given away our gold,' her mother wailed into the night. And the wind picked up her words and carried them into the farthest corners of Ireland and into the cave where Padraig, and his father Diarmuid, were snoozing beside a nice fire after another fruitless day of searching for the other lost gold.

'Did you hear anything?' Padraig said to his father.

'I heard the wind whistle and a log settling in the fire and your mother snoring in the corner. What did you hear?'

'I fancied that I heard my wife's voice in the wind. I imagined that she said Biddy had given away our gold.'

'Never!' Diarmuid said. 'I'll give it to you that the girl is a bit of a fool, but no leprechaun since time began has ever willingly given away a pot of gold. She wouldn't do it. Isn't she your own flesh and blood?'

'Just the same,' said Padraig. 'I'd better go and check it out.'

And with that they both got up, leaving the nice warm fire and the snoring grandmother to go out into the bleak night.

'Biddy, daughter of Padraig, granddaughter of Diarmuid, has given away a pot of gold,' every leprechaun throughout the county echoed. And one by one they left their fireplaces and converged on the hill above the stone cottage. Together, like an army, they marched down the hill and rapped loudly on the door.

Silence.

'Search the house!' Padraig said, pushing open the door. 'Leave no scone unturned.'

Leprechauns of every size and description filled the small house. They pulled out drawers, upended beds, lifted floorboards, shifted turf, tasted bacon, quenched the fire that hadn't been out for fifty years and crawled up the chimney, but they didn't find the gold.

It was to this chaotic scene that Corey's father and grandfather returned.

'What is the meaning of this?' Corey's father bellowed. 'How dare you wreck my father's house, you cowardly midgets.'

'Shhh!' said Corey's grandfather. 'Don't upset them with name calling.'

'Don't upset them?' Corey's father said, his face red with rage. 'Where is my son? What have you done with Corey?'

'Corey?' echoed hundreds of voices. 'What kind of name is that?'

'We've heard of Connor and Cathal and Conan and Cromwell, but not Corey. What does it mean?'

'It means thief,' Padraig said. 'Your son has stolen our gold.'

'Rubbish!' said Corey's father.

'Heaven help us,' said Corey's grandfather, blessing himself. 'I knew the boy was up to no good.'

'What d'you mean?'

'He came down the hill last week with a bundle under his oxter and I knew he was up to something.'

'Don't be ridiculous,' Corey's father said. 'I won't believe it. Corey would never steal anything.'

'Ask him yourself then,' said Biddy, who had just noticed Corey arriving outside the house on the bicycle.

'Ask me what?' Corey walked in, quite cool now that the gold was safe.

'Did you steal our gold?' Biddy's mother pushed Corey into a corner and prodded him in the stomach. (That was as high as she could reach.)

'Course I didn't,' Corey scoffed. 'It was a fair deal, all legal and above board,' he said, imitating his father, who was a very important lawyer.

'Legal and above board?' The leprechauns repeated.

'Biddy, give an account of yourself,' her mother demanded.

'She said she'd swap the gold for a week of sunshine,' Corey explained before Biddy could open her mouth. 'So I gave her a week of sunshine. She can't deny it either because that sunburn is a dead giveaway.'

'I did not say I'd swap the gold!' Biddy contradicted.

'Dirty liar, you did,' Corey yelled.

'Well, exactly what did you say then?' the leprechauns demanded, gathering around Biddy who was now in the centre of a large circle.

'I was alone on the hillside one day, minding my own business, talking to myself,' Biddy explained. 'I was miserable from the wetness of the rain and the weight of my father's gold and I said, if I could, I would trade the gold for a week of sunshine. Suddenly this boy hopped out of a blackthorn tree and offered me a week of sunshine. So, to cut a long story short, I left him to mind the gold while I was away, but I borrowed his passport to make sure he'd give it back when I returned.'

'You gave away your passport?' Corey's father was shocked. 'I'm surprised at you, Son. Where is it now?'

'She lost it,' Corey pointed at Biddy.

'I did not!' Biddy said. 'I just can't remember where I put it.'

'Just like her grandfather,' a few of the leprechauns nudged each other.

'Enough!' Padraig roared. 'Where is my gold?'

'Safe,' Corey said. 'I buried it.'

A loud groan filled the house.

'You buried it! You fool! Where did you bury it?' they all yelled.

'Somewhere!' Corey said, staying remarkably cool for someone surrounded by leprechauns. 'And I'm not giving it back. The gold is mine now. You can't do anything about it.'

'Can't we?' said Padraig, his face trembling with temper. 'Just wait and see what we can do.'

And with that they picked up Corey's grandfather and marched off up the hill with him.

'You'll get your grandfather back when you return the gold,' they said, disappearing into the blackest night you've ever seen and leaving Corey alone to face his father.

10. How Corey Learned a Few Home Truths

'This is a terrible state of affairs!'

Corey's father shook his head in disbelief as he looked at the mess – the broken crockery, the upended chairs, the pictures hanging skew-wiff on the walls. 'What have you got to say for yourself, Son?'

'We can clean it up,' Corey suggested. 'At least we've still got the gold, Dad. We're rich! You always wanted to be rich and now you can have that new speedboat you liked so much and I can have anything I want. All we have to do is melt the gold into nuggets and sell it.'

'Is that what you really believe?' Corey's father looked up. His eyes seemed wide and dark and moist. 'Do you really think that there is any joy to be had in taking things without earning them? And what about your grandfather?'

'We'll get him back somehow,' Corey said in an undertone, not wanting to admit that he hadn't thought much about his grandfather's welfare. 'They won't hurt him. They're only interested in the gold, same as us.'

'You've got a lot to learn, Son,' his father said. 'Everything I own I've worked hard for and I wouldn't have it any other way. I don't want their gold. Now let's go to bed. We'll have to get up very early in the morning to sort out this whole mess.'

Corey didn't sleep. He watched the sky outside the small room lighten gradually to reveal another grey day. His father didn't sleep much either. Corey could tell by the sighs in his breathing and by the cold silence which swirled like an incoming tide around and underneath his bed.

'Well, what are you going to do?' his father asked as they ate dry lumps of bread, because the fire which hadn't been quenched for fifty years stubbornly refused to light and cook breakfast for them.

'Go and dig up the gold, I suppose,' Corey answered sullenly, bitter at having to return his treasure.

'Good boy!' his father smiled. 'I knew I could depend on you to make the right decision. You'll feel much better when you return it.'

Not likely! Corey thought. Only two things would make me feel better. One, I'd like to give Biddy Blatherskate a black eye for messing everything up and especially for losing my passport. Two, I'd like to keep the gold.

'Well, off with you then,' his father said cheerfully. 'I don't like the look of those clouds. You'd better dig up the gold before it starts raining. While you're away I'll ring the airport about your passport.'

Corey hopped on his bicycle. He pedalled slowly down the lane, past the shops and past the church until he reached the graveyard. Pushing past the rusty iron gate, he walked as far as the angel with the broken wing, then counted five graves to the right and started digging.

To his relief the gold was still there. He took it to a tap, located just inside the gate, and washed the dirt off. The gold looked shinier than ever.

'I can't give it up, ' he told himself, filling his hands with coins and allowing them to slip through his fingers into the pot.

Quickly he wrapped the pot in his jacket and cycled to the hardware store. There, he bought two big boxes of washers and a tin of quick-drying gold paint. Then he popped into the newsagents and bought a newspaper.

Back at the graveyard, concealed behind a hedge, Corey spread the newspaper on the ground, anchoring the edges with rocks. Then he spread all the washers out and painted them. The sky was darkening. He had to hurry.

Next he emptied all of the gold into his jacket. As soon as the washers were dry he half-filled the pot and topped it up with real gold. Well, half a pot of gold was better than none at all, he thought. He lifted the pot. The weight was almost the same. Nobody would know about the washers, not until he was long gone, anyway.

There was still the problem of his half of the

gold. He couldn't really bury it, because there might not be time to dig it up again. He couldn't just wrap it in his jacket and carry it in the basket of the bicycle because someone was sure to discover it. He had to find some way to conceal it.

Then he had an idea.

He pulled off his boots, went to the tap, mixed up a nice thick mud pie, kneaded all the gold coins into it, then filled his boots with the mixture and pushed his stripey socks in on top. Now he smeared some mud around the outsides. The gold didn't rattle and the boots looked too filthy to be touched by anyone.

Happy with his plan, Corey cleaned himself up, placed the pot of gold, his boots and his jacket into the basket of the bicycle and cycled back to the cottage.

Biddy was there, sitting on the doorstep, her chin in her hands.

'Did you find my gold?' she demanded.

'Did you find my passport?' Corey snapped.

'Yeah! It was in my pocket all the time. It fell through a hole in the lining, that's all.' She pulled the crumpled document out.

'I'll take that!' Corey's father snatched the passport. 'Now give her the gold, Corey. We haven't got any time to waste if we're to catch our plane.'

'Where's Grandfather?' Corey asked before passing over the pot of gold.

'Up there.' Biddy pointed at the hillside and there, sure enough, like an army in disarray, were the leprechauns. 'Goodbye so,' Biddy said. 'I can't say it was much fun meeting you.'

'Ditto!' Corey said, kicking his heel against the doorstep.

'What happened to your boots?' Corey's father frowned.

'I had to take them off cos they got muddy.'

'Is that a fact?' Biddy squinted against a sudden ray of sunlight.

'Shouldn't you be going now?' Corey demanded. 'We've got to get to the airport, so we want Grandfather back in a hurry.'

Biddy hitched the pot on to her hip and set off. Once or twice along the way she stopped to change its position and Corey felt his heart beat wildly in case she had noticed something. Then she went on again.

Soon there was wild yahooing and singing and dancing on the hillside. The place echoed with the sound of it.

Corey's grandfather arrived, puffing and panting and looking decidedly unimpressed.

'You young pup!' he said to Corey. 'Didn't I tell you not to mess with the little people. It's a lucky day for us that you returned the gold or they'd be dancing around our dead bodies.'

'It's all right!' Corey's father said. 'I think Corey has learned his lesson. Haven't you, Son?'

'Yes, Dad!' Corey said. 'Maybe you should make Grandad a nice cup of tea while I clean my boots.'

'I'll make my own tea,' Grandfather snapped.

Corey took his boots to the shed. He found a cloth and cleaned the outsides. There was no way he could get the gold out, not with his father prowling around and his grandfather so hostile and suspicious. He'd have to take them back to Australia as they were, mud and all.

He found a plastic bag and placed the boots in there, then managed to get them upstairs and into his suitcase. With clothes and towels wrapped around them they were hardly noticeable.

The gold was safe. Corey took the suitcase downstairs. His father had already placed the rest of the luggage in the doorway. Corey hoped the taxi would arrive soon, before the leprechauns discovered that half of their gold was gone.

'You've really got ants in your pants, haven't you?' his father said. 'Come on inside and say goodbye to your grandfather.'

The taxi arrived. The suitcases were safely stowed away in the boot. The three men stood on the doorstep chatting while Corey hopped from one foot to the other and glanced nervously up the hill. Once he thought that something moved but then it disappeared again.

He climbed into the back of the taxi. His father and the driver hopped into the front. His grandfather's face looked as solid as the stones in the garden wall.

The laneway, the cottage and the old man disappeared in a cloud of dust. Corey exhaled and sank back into the car seat. Safe at last. Now to get out of the country as fast as possible.

11. How Biddy was Banished

For three days the leprechauns sang and danced and celebrated. Nothing pleased them more than to regain a lost pot of gold. Music tripped from their violins. Sparks flew from the toes of their dancing shoes. The light of happiness from their eyes added a new sparkle to the stars in the sky over the mountain where they had congregated for a great feast.

For the whole of the first day Biddy sat apart from everyone. She wasn't exactly in leprechaun jail but there was a wall of hostile silence around her, made more unbearable by the barbs of snide remarks which occasionally reached her ears. To make matters worse, her mother had snatched the gold from her and given it to her father right in front of everyone.

'You'll never guard the gold again,' she said. 'You're too irresponsible.'

'She's as scatterbrained as her grandfather,' some of the older leprechauns whispered.

'She can't see past that Blatherskate nose,' some of the younger ones sniggered.

'I don't give a sheep's bleat!' Biddy muttered from her uncomfortable spot on a large rock. 'I don't give a nanny goat's nob if I never set eyes on another pot of gold.'

But she did. It irked her to see her cousins proudly polishing their gold, comparing coins. It went right up her very long nose to see them perched on their pots, shifting around trying to find a comfortable spot. Biddy knew just how uncomfortable it was, and in a way she kind of missed that discomfort.

She watched as they all guzzled dandelion wine and stuffed their mouths with roasted rabbit and boiled potatoes bursting like spring flowers from their skins. She listened to their silly, boring stories, about how they had protected their gold from thieves and robbers.

'But you've never been inside the great winged

birds that roar across the sky,' she said, as she shuffled a bit closer on the second day.

'Shut your gob!' they said. 'Go back to your rock.'

'I don't have to,' Biddy said.

'We don't talk to gold losers,' they said.

'It doesn't matter,' Biddy said. 'I've been to places you'll never visit. I've seen sights you'll never see.'

'Tell us and we'll decide if it's true or not.'

'Nah!' Biddy said then. 'I'd rather die than tell you anything.'

But by then the leprechauns were getting tired of singing and dancing and if their belts had to be loosened any more they'd all lose their pants. Now it was time to be entertained, to hear stories from afar. So they threw a few more sods of turf on the fire and gathered in a big circle, their hands clasped around their knees.

'Come on, Biddy, me darlin,' Biddy's grandfather always developed a happier disposition when he had consumed several tumblers of his wife's special brew. 'Speak to us of your travels. Redeem yourself.'

Biddy wasn't backward about coming forward. She didn't have to be asked twice. She flew around the fire like a jumbo jet, roaring to give them an idea of how the engines sounded.

'And we got food in that plane the likes of which you'd never see in Ireland,' she told them.

'Like what?' They asked.

'Like shiny black eyeballs, and green ones with red pupils.'

'Ugh!' They groaned. 'What did they taste like?'

'Bitter as bog water,' she said. 'And glasses of blood to wash them down.'

'Tell us about Australia,' they begged.

'It's bigger than imagination,' she almost whispered, because by then there wasn't a sound to be heard except for the crackling of the fire. 'They have a sun monster who goes around burning skin by day. And at night tiny spirits buzz in your ear and while you're busy slapping yourself on the head they stick a sharp needle into another part of your body.'

'Where on your body?'

'Anywhere, everywhere.'

'What else?'

'The aliens burn their food outside on bits of steel and inside they eat Vegemite which smells like ...'

'Like what?'

'Well, actually,' Biddy glanced around.' It's very pungent, like my grandfather's socks.'

'Biddy!' her mother said sharply.

'And it never, ever, ever rains there. It's as dry as a thirsty throat from one end of the week to the next and the water is too vile to swallow.'

By the end of the night Biddy was a hero. To her stories she added new monsters, new food, new aliens the likes of which she'd never even seen herself.

On the third day the pot of gold was returned to her.

'Guard it with your life,' her father, who was already sick of looking after it, said. 'If anything happens to it your mother will throttle me.'

Biddy was delighted. She pranced with it and danced with it and decided that she would become the best gold minder in the leprechaun world. She would even personally count every single coin in the pot.

She found a quiet spot out of the wind and started stacking the gold coins into piles. For every pile of ten she cut a notch in a piece of stick with her father's best knife. By dusk she'd counted half the gold. She'd never been that far before.

'Holey gold!' she exclaimed with delight when she got to the painted washers. 'Oh, this is nice gold,' she exclaimed. 'If I put it on a string I could wear it around my waist and then the pot wouldn't be as heavy to carry.'

So that's just what she did. She found some twine and threaded it through the gold washers. She hung one strand around her waist, one around her neck and a few on her wrists. Then she danced and twirled her way back to the party with her half pot of gold.

'Biddy! What are you doing?' her mother demanded.

'I'm thinking that if Dad could make holes in the rest of the gold I could wear it all and never lose it again.'

'Holes in the gold?' every leprechaun in the place echoed.

'Holes in the gold?' Her father leapt to his feet.

'What d'you mean, make holes in the gold?'

'Like this gold!' Biddy pulled up her jumper and pushed up her sleeves.

'Where did you get it?' her mother looked fierce.

'In the pot, of course,' Biddy explained. 'I was counting it.'

'You little fool! You little twit! You've been tricked by that alien. This is not gold!' Her mother yanked at the string and a whole stream of washers fell into the fire. The paint burned off.

Biddy felt sick.

So, that was why Corey wasn't wearing his boots. She'd thought it strange that his bicycle tyres were clean when his boots were so muddy. Now she knew why.

'Oh, I really am stupid,' she cried, tearing off the rest of the washers and flinging them into the fire.

'Let Biddy Blatherskate's blunder be written into the history books as a warning to future generations,' the oldest leprechaun said. 'Let Biddy Blatherskate be banished from this kingdom until she returns the gold.'

'GO! GO! GO!' The rest of the leprechauns started chanting and Biddy, with tears streaming down her cheeks, ran off into one of the blackest nights ever seen over that part of the mountain.

12. How Biddy Found a New Home

Biddy didn't go far that night. Darkness as thick as burnt treacle made progress over the mountain so hazardous that after falling several times, grazing her knees and elbows, she finally crawled under the shelter of a large rock, curled into a tight ball and cried herself to sleep.

In the morning the sun, as bleary eyed as herself, came sluggishly over the horizon, took one look around, then disappeared under a blanket of thick grey cloud and stayed there.

Biddy crept out from under the sheltering rock, shook herself a few times to get her blood circulating, then started walking down the hill towards the valley where Corey's grandfather lived.

'What brings you here?' the grandfather asked when he opened the door in answer to Biddy's loud knocking. 'If you've lost the gold again you're looking in the wrong place for it, because I wouldn't touch leprechaun gold with a ten-metre nose ... pole, I mean,' he added, trying not to stare at Biddy's nose, which seemed longer and more bulbous than ever after all the crying. 'And that young pup, Corey, is gone back to Australia, so there's no point in blaming him either.'

'Isn't there now?' Biddy sniffed. 'He tricked me. He put useless washers in our pot and stole half of our gold. I've been banished until I find and return the other half.'

'Is that a fact?' The old man gazed off into the distance, his eyes narrow, his lips tight. 'You'd better come inside then and have a bite to eat, I suppose,' he said.

'All right so!' Biddy brightened up a bit at the prospect of food.

The tip of Biddy's nose wriggled at the enticing smell of sizzling rashers and black puddings and her eyes sparkled at the sight of egg yolks as yellow as new daffodils.

'I don't know what the alien was complaining about,' she said, after eating every scrap of food on her plate. 'That's the finest food I've eaten in ages. You don't mind if I lick the grease from the plate, do you?'

'Be my guest,' the grandfather said, though he didn't know how she was going to manage it with a nose so large and swollen. Biddy managed admirably and afterwards wiped her nose and cheeks on the sleeve of her cardigan.

'Delicious!' she said, patting her stomach and stretching out on the stool like a cat with a bellyful of rats. 'I could live here with you for a while,' she announced.

'No! That wouldn't do at all.' The grandfather looked alarmed. He tapped his fingers on the table and a red flush came into his cheeks.

'Why not?' asked Biddy. 'Your grandson got me thrown out of home. I have to live somewhere and here is as good a place as any.' *Better than some*, she thought, thinking of how her mother always burned the potatoes and put too much salt in the cabbage. 'I'll be no trouble at all,' she assured the old man. 'I'll collect firewood for you and run errands. In twenty or thirty years my family might cool down a bit and let me go home.'

'Twenty or thirty years!' yelped the grandfather. 'I'll be dead and buried and pushing up daisies in twenty or thirty years.'

'Don't worry,' Biddy said. 'I'll look after the place when you're dead and gone, won't that be nice?'

'Oh, very nice indeed,' he said, spitting into the fire. 'Just what I need, a leprechaun living under my own roof,' he muttered under his breath.

'That's settled then,' Biddy sprang up. 'Which room is mine?' And without waiting for an answer she bolted up the rickety stairs, prancing and dancing about in the rooms up there, making all the floor boards creak and moan and making the grandfather, below stairs, shriek and groan.

'What ever will I do?' he said to the flickering flames in his fireplace. 'Oil and water don't mix. Either she'll be the death of me or I'll be the death of her.' And he put his head in his hands and worried for the rest of the day.

That night, when Biddy was asleep in bed, he wrote an urgent note to his grandson:

Corey,

The leprechaun knows about the gold. She's been banished from leprechaun land and is here living under my own roof, tormenting the life out of me. Have pity on me. Return the gold and we'll say no more about the whole sorry affair.

Your grandfather.

After two weeks a small scribbled note came from Australia:

Grandfather,

I don't know what you're talking about. That leprechaun is an awful liar. Don't believe anything she tells you. Didn't you see me returning the gold yourself? Chuck her out.

Corey.

'He's the liar!' Biddy screamed when the grandfather read the note. 'I've a good mind to go to Australia and belt the living daylights out of him.'

'Go on then,' the grandfather said. 'I'd like to give him a thick ear myself, but I can't afford the airfare.'

'Would you indeed?' said Biddy. 'Don't tempt me. I'd go tomorrow if it wasn't for the sun monster.'

'I didn't think leprechauns were such scaredy-cats,' the grandfather said. Having to put up with Biddy eating him out of house and home had made him a bit more daring that he would normally have been.

'Leprechauns are not scaredy-cats,' Biddy snapped. She was getting sick of the old man. He was no fun at all to live with. Every day he just smoked his pipe and gazed into the fireplace. Every day there was less food in the larder and he was refusing to buy more.

'Leprechauns are strong and smart and cunning,' Biddy announced irritably, stamping her foot hard on the floor.

'Not as strong and smart and cunning as my grandson,' the old man replied. 'He tricked you out of the gold. I'd have to say that he's got more backbone than you've got.'

Biddy was furious. She stomped up the stairs and jumped on the spring mattress for hours while trying to come up with some awful way to deal with the cranky old man. When she came down that night there was absolutely nothing for dinner.

'Aren't you hungry?' Biddy demanded.

'Not a bit!' the old man said cheerfully. He'd been digging in the vegetable garden all afternoon and had eaten his fill of raw carrots and tomatoes and had swallowed two raw eggs for dessert.

Biddy slammed the larder door. 'Humans are ridiculous creatures,' she said. 'Get me something to eat or I'll cripple you.'

'I'm crippled already,' the old man said. 'If that's the worst you can do then I've nothing to fear. Anyway, I've written Corey's address on an old envelope in case you change your mind about reclaiming your gold,' he said. 'It's there on the table.'

And with that he made his way to bed, leaving Biddy by the fireplace to nurse an empty stomach and a very bad temper.

13. How Corey had New Problems

Corey burned his grandfather's letter.

'Phew! Lucky for me that Dad wasn't here to collect the mail,' he said as he scooped the ashes into the rubbish bin.

'What are you up to?' demanded Cordelia, the new housekeeper.

'Mind your own beeswax,' Corey mumbled. He didn't like Cordelia. She was bossy and nosy and he was really angry with his father for having hired her.

To make matters worse, Cordelia had a son who was the same age as Corey. They were living in the granny flat over the garage, snooping around all the time, swimming in the pool, prancing around on the tennis court, and if that wasn't bad enough, Angela Morris liked the little twit. 'He's so cute!' she said the first day he arrived at Corey's school. Now Corey was desperate to get rid of both of them.

'What did you say?' Cordelia asked.

'Nothing!' Corey answered. 'Just mending something with beeswax.'

'That's all right then,' she said. 'I wouldn't take any impudence from you, that's all.'

'No!' Corey said.

In some ways Cordelia scared him. She was a small woman, but there was something quite fierce about her. She reminded Corey of a death adder, coiled, just waiting for a chance to spring at him.

'Old Witch!' he mumbled as he walked away.

In his bedroom, with the door locked, Corey wondered what to do about the gold. It had been difficult to conceal ever since he'd left Ireland. For a start, the customs officer had nearly sprung it at Brisbane Airport.

Then, when his father had seen the muddy boots he went berserk.

'Totally irresponsible!' he yelled. 'Do you realise the danger of bringing that sort of material into the country? You could be responsible for introducing new pests and diseases into Australia. Give them to me, I'll put them into the incinerator immediately.'

Fortunately for Corey, the telephone rang at that moment and his father was occupied for some time. 'I'll do it,' Corey said, racing outside to rescue the gold before burning his good boots.

Still Corey was angry with his father for speaking to him the way he spoke to clients in the courtroom, as if he was a criminal. Then, a week later, this new housekeeper had arrived, as if Corey wasn't capable of looking after himself.

'It will be nice for you to have some company when I'm not around,' his father said. But having the housekeeper and her son around was the last thing Corey wanted and their presence in the house was making the secret of the gold harder to conceal.

'Dad must never find out about it,' Corey muttered as he paced about the bedroom. 'I'll just have to hide it somewhere Cordelia won't even think of dusting.'

14. How It Ended

After the old man had gone to bed, Biddy sat, spitting into the fire. She couldn't go to bed, not with such an empty stomach. She found a cardboard cereal box and ate half of that, then washed it down with the dregs from the milk jug.

'I wish I could go home to my mother,' she moaned. 'I hate living with this horrible, stinky old human. I miss my mother's awful cooking, and my untidy bed, and I miss looking after my father's gold.'

With that, she snatched up the envelope with Corey's address on it and stuck it in her pocket. Just as the sun was rising, she let herself out of the house and walked down the laneway. 'I will reclaim my gold,' she said. 'I'm a leprechaun and I won't be defeated.'

It was raining when Biddy arrived in Brisbane. She caught a bus to the city and hung around the Queen Street Mall. She liked it there, plenty of shade, plenty of food. For two days she stuffed herself. On the third day she pulled the envelope out of her pocket and asked directions to Morningside.

'I'm going there myself,' an old woman said. 'Just follow me if you like.'

Finding the right street was more difficult. Biddy walked and walked for hours until there were blisters on the soles of her feet. She was just about to give up, to search for somewhere comfortable to sleep when she saw, in the distance, a familiar haystack-type of head.

'The alien! The thief!' she gasped. 'Right under my nose. If he was a dog I'd have tripped over him. And what is he up to?' she wondered to herself, because he seemed to be pushing something like a small bundle of clothes into a hedge.

When she got closer she saw that the bundle of clothes had a body and was squealing, 'Let me go or I'll dob you in to my mother.'

94

'Dob me in and I'll beat you twice as hard tomorrow.'

Seeing Corey again made Biddy incredibly angry. Thinking of the way he'd tricked her made her insides hot, and watching him bullying a smaller human made her furious, so furious that she ran towards him and leapt on to his back. They both stumbled and fell headlong into a flower garden.

'Biddy! Is that really you?' the body in the bundle of clothes gasped.

'Torren! Surely it can't be you?' Biddy panted.

'How come you two creeps know each other?' Corey wiped the dust from his clothes.

'None of your business,' Biddy said. 'I've come for my gold and I'm not going home until you hand it over.'

'I don't know what you're talking about.' Corey turned his back and walked away. 'I haven't got your stupid gold.'

Back in the granny flat, Torren made Biddy a honey sandwich and a chocolate milkshake.

'But why are you living in Brisbane with the alien?' she asked.

'My mother saw this job advertisement and we needed the money,' Torren said sadly. 'But I don't like it here. I miss the sea and I miss my friends and I hate Corey.'

'Me too!' Biddy told Torren about the gold.

'I'll bet it's in his bedroom,' Torren said. 'He's always got the door locked.'

'When I get the gold back I'll share it with you so that you can go back to Hervey Bay,' Biddy said. 'I don't think my parents will miss a handful of coins.'

'Thanks!' Torren said. 'I'll ask my mother to help us.'

'I'll have a look tomorrow while Corey's at school,' Cordelia promised when she heard the whole story. 'We'll sort something out.'

'I'll help you look,' Biddy said.

But Corey didn't go to school.

'I've got a stomach ache,' he told his father. 'The housekeeper is trying to poison me with the awful food she cooks.'

'Don't be ridiculous!' Corey's father said. 'But you'd better stay in bed for the day anyway. I've got to go away for a few days but I'll ring every night.'

For three days Corey didn't come out of his room. Biddy paced about in the granny flat. On Saturday morning Biddy and Torren crept upstairs to Corey's room and knocked lightly on the door.

'Breakfast, Dear!' cooed Biddy, sounding just like Cordelia.

Corey opened the door. Biddy and Torren pushed past him into the room. Then they turned around and pushed Corey out into the hallway, locking the door behind him.

'Let me in!' Corey banged on the door.

'What's going on?' Corey's father stumbled out of his room. He looked sleepy.

'Oh! I didn't know you were home,' Corey said. 'Sorry about the noise, Dad, it's just a few friends messing about.'

Cordelia stepped out of the shadows. 'That's not quite true, Mr Sullivan. I know this is probably going to sound far-fetched. You'll probably think I'm crazy, but there's a leprechaun in there looking for ...'

'Some gold, perhaps?' Corey's father finished the sentence. 'Corey, you don't still have some of that gold, do you?'

'Course not! The leprechaun's lying.'

'Well, you won't mind if we have a look in your room then, will you?'

Torren opened the door.

'Hello, Biddy!' Mr Sullivan said, although he looked far from pleased to see her standing there with her hands on her hips.

'I just want my gold and I'll be off,' Biddy said, knowing that she wasn't welcome.

Corey's father searched the room. He emptied out closets, turned the mattress on the bed, shifted all the books on the bookshelf, but he didn't find the gold.

'Perhaps you're mistaken, Biddy,' he said.

'Indeed, I'm not,' she stamped her foot for emphasis. 'He brought the gold to Australia in his boots.'

'Ah! The boots, was it?' Corey's father stroked his chin thoughtfully. 'Biddy, I think you could be right. The muddy boots.'

'It's not true, I tell you,' Corey said. 'She's lying.'

'I am not!' Biddy was so angry that she rushed at Corey and pushed him against the wardrobe.

The wardrobe wobbled. A row of stuffed toys on top of the wardrobe tilted forward and fell off. A pink, fluffy elephant hit Corey on the head and knocked him to the ground.

'You've killed him,' Torren gasped.

'Don't be ridiculous! How could anyone be killed by a stuffed toy?' Cordelia grabbed the elephant. 'It is incredibly heavy for a soft toy,' she said. 'As heavy as a lump of lead.'

'As heavy as half a pot of gold, perhaps?' Biddy grabbed the elephant and ripped it open. Gold coins spilled everywhere.

Corey sat up. 'What happened?' He rubbed his head and looked a bit dazed.

'Your son is a liar and a cheat,' Biddy said.

'And a bully,' Torren added.

'And bad tempered and rude,' Cordelia finished. 'I don't think I can work for you any longer, Mr Sullivan.'

Corey's father sat on the bed. 'I'm afraid you're all right,' he said sadly. 'I just didn't want to believe these things were happening. Have you got anything to say, Son?'

Corey shrugged his shoulders.

'I think all of these people deserve an apology.'

'Sorry!' Corey muttered, not sounding at all apologetic.

'We have a lot of talking to do,' Mr Sullivan said. 'Perhaps you'd better leave now.'

'Not before I give Corey a parting gift,' Biddy said.

'What?' Torren whispered.

'I think I'll make his fingers longer and his thumbs so short that he'll always have trouble picking up other people's coins,' Biddy said thoughtfully.

Torren giggled nervously. 'Can you really do that?'

'Course I can.'

'Stop her, Dad!' Corey crept closer to his father. 'Don't let her do it.'

'She's not going to do anything, Son.'

'He's got to be punished,' Biddy said. 'It's the law of the leprechauns.'

'Then change the law, Biddy,' Mr Sullivan said.

'Two wrongs don't make a right.'

'That's true,' Cordelia agreed.

'Torren, what do you think?' Biddy asked. 'Corey beats you up every afternoon on the way home from school. 'Don't you want to punish him?'

'I just want him to stop picking on me,' Torren said.

'Leave Corey to me,' Mr Sullivan said, showing everyone to the door. 'I promise you that we'll work something out.'

'Goodbye so!' Biddy gathered up her gold and left reluctantly. 'Goodbye!'

15. How the End was Just
a New Beginning

For a long time after everyone had gone, Mr Sullivan sat on the end of Corey's bed. He chewed his lip and looked out the window and sometimes nodded his head. Corey had never seen his father behave like this before. In fact, he didn't see his father much at all, because Mr Sullivan was a very busy lawyer and was always away somewhere working on important cases. Even when he was at home he spent most of his time in the study making telephone calls or researching. Occasionally, he and Corey took a holiday together, but even then they were usually with other people.

Corey didn't mind most of the time. He had a television in his room and a computer with lots of games. He ate what he liked and went to bed whenever he chose to. His friends thought he was lucky.

'Corey,' his father said after a long time.

Corey tensed up, waiting for the lecture he was sure his father had been rehearsing. 'What?' he asked sulkily.

'Things are going to have to change around here,' his father said.

I knew it, Corey thought. I suppose he's going to ground me for the rest of my life. Well, who cares?

'I'm glad this business with the gold happened.'

'You are?' Corey was amazed.

'Yes! It's made me sit up and take notice. Do you know what we're going to do?'

'What?' Corey couldn't imagine what his father wanted to do.

'We're going to sell this big house and go on a trip around Australia together.'

'But what about school?'

'You can do correspondence. I'll teach you.'

'But what about your work?'

'I think I've been working too much,' Mr

Sullivan said. 'I'm just as bad as the leprechauns. I've been guarding the wrong treasures. It's time we two really got to know each other.'

'Can we get a boat and go fishing?' Corey was on his knees. There was a new light of excitement in his eyes.

'Certainly,' his father said. 'I'll ring the estate agent right away. You can go to the garage and dig out those old fishing rods we never got around to using before.'

Corey leapt off the bed and ran to the door. He stopped suddenly, and looked back at his father with a troubled expression in his eyes. 'You're not going to change your mind are you, Dad, like ...?'

'Like I've always done before? No, Corey. This time there will be no backing down.'

'Cool!' Corey said. 'I can't wait to tell Angela Morris.' And he ran down the stairs, his haystack bobbing around on top of his head.

Biddy helped Cordelia and Torren to pack their belongings into the old car. She was glad that Torren was going back to the sea because she knew what it was like to miss home, how sounds and smells and voices reminded you of things absent.

'I suppose you're going straight back to Ireland,' Cordelia said. 'I expect your parents will be worried about you.'

'They only worry about the gold,' Biddy said, thinking how lucky Torren was to have such a friendly mother.

'I'm sure that's not true,' Cordelia said.

'I'm sure it is,' Biddy answered. 'Anyway, I thought I might hang around for a few days. I want to see a kangaroo and get some new stories to take back with me. I'm the only leprechaun that's ever been in Australia. I'm going to be famous.'

'Can't she come home with us for a while,' Torren asked. 'There's a spare bed in my room.'

'Would you like to do that, Biddy?' Cordelia asked.

'I would indeed,' Biddy said. 'As long as it's not too much trouble.'

'That's settled then.' Cordelia put the last suitcase into the back of the car and shut the door. 'Let's go,' she said.

Biddy hopped into the front of the car. It had a bench seat, so she plonked herself in the middle, her bag of gold on her knees. Torren hopped in beside her. Cordelia turned the key in the ignition.

Corey came running out of the house at that moment. He looked different, a sweet half-orange face instead of a bitter one. He was heading towards the garage, occasionally stopping to leap into the air and kick an imaginary opponent.

'Were you really going to do those awful things to his hands?' Torren asked.

'Not at all,' Biddy giggled. 'I just wanted to frighten the pants off him, that's all.'

'I thought so. You're not bad for a leprechaun,' Torren said.

'Nor you, for an alien,' Biddy replied, snuggling into the car seat. 'Can you mind this gold for a while?' she said, planting the bag on Torren's knee. 'I get kind of sick of looking after it all the time.'

'We could put it the bank until you're ready to go home,' Cordelia offered.

'Forget it!' Biddy snatched the bag back and sat on it.

'Isn't that uncomfortable?' Cordelia chuckled.

'You get used to it,' Biddy said, squirming around to find the right spot.

'I expect you can get used to anything after a while,' Cordelia smiled at Torren over the top of Biddy's head. 'Even strange creatures from other lands.'

'Like humans, you mean?' Biddy yawned and put her head against Cordelia's shoulder.

'I was thinking more of leprechauns.' Cordelia turned to wink at Torren but he was already asleep, his head propped against the window of the car, a contented smile on his face.

Annette Kelleher

Annette Kelleher was hatched on the side of a cliff on Kenmare Bay. As soon as she could crawl, she fell over the edge of the cliff, but was saved from certain death by a low-flying eagle, who deposited her on the doorstep of a flesh-eating monster on Mangerton Mountain.

However, this baby was so ugly that every time the monster tried to eat her he got incredibly nauseous, so eventually he kept her to do useful things like fly-swatting, midge-swallowing and eating his ugly toenails, which grew an inch a day.

One day she escaped and was adopted by a group of leprechauns, which is why Annette Kelleher knows so much about the wonderful little people.

Class No. ___J9-11___ Acc No. _C/148880_

Author: _Kelleher, A_ Loc: _____

1. **This book may be kept three weeks. It is to be returned on / before the last date stamped below.**

2. **A fine of 25c will** ~~be~~ ~~ch~~ **y week or part of we**

I / C148880

~ 9 NOV 2006

1 6 JAN 2008